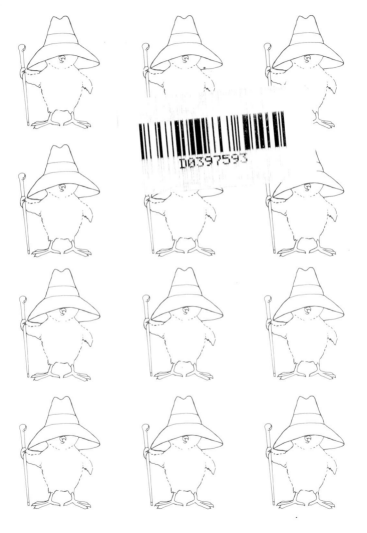

D0397593

LITTLE OWL'S
Favorite Uncle

Constance Boyle

Woodbury, New York · London · Toronto · Sydney

First U.S. edition published in 1985
by Barron's Educational Series, Inc.

© Constance Boyle 1985

This book has been designed and produced by
Aurum Press Limited,
33 Museum Street, London WC1A 1LD, England.

All inquiries should be addressed to:
Barron's Educational Series, Inc.
113 Crossways Park Drive
Woodbury, New York 11797

International Standard Book No. 0-8120-5675-2
Library of Congress Catalog Card No. 85-9204

PRINTED IN BELGIUM

5 4 3   9 8 7 6 5 4 3 2 1

Little Owl had always liked Uncle
Horace.

It was Uncle Horace who had given
Little Owl his teddy bear, the best
present he had ever had.

When Uncle
Horace told
stories, the whole
family stopped to
listen, even Little
Owl's noisy
brother Olly.

Uncle Horace wore a rather unusual hat, and a floppy bow tie . . .

and he had a black cane with a silver knob.

Little Owl
especially liked the
hat. One day, he
managed to climb
up and get it down
from the hook.

When he tried it on, he couldn't see very well, and everyone laughed.
"You like my hat, do you?" asked Uncle Horace.

They waved to Uncle Horace when he left.

"Why DOES Uncle Horace wear that funny hat?" asked Olly.

"Oh, he's an actor," said Daddy. "He always liked dressing-up."

Little Owl wondered what an actor was.

When they went back into the house Daddy showed them some photographs of Uncle Horace when he was Olly's age.

Little Owl was very surprised to see a gypsy, and a pirate . . .

and a very pretty
young lady.
"That CAN'T be
Uncle Horace!"
shouted Olly.

He laughed so much that he fell on the
floor.

They didn't see Uncle Horace again
until Olly's birthday.
He took them out in a boat.

Olly enjoyed it enormously!

Then, one day, a
very large package
arrived for Daddy.

Little Owl and his mother wondered
what it could be.

Daddy opened the package when he came home. "This is great!" he said. "Horace has sent us our old puppet theater! He used to love this when we were boys."

"Look! It's Uncle Horace!" said Little Owl, holding up a puppet with dark feathers.

"He hasn't got a hat!" said Olly. "Shall I make him one?" asked Mommy. Little Owl nodded. "AND a floppy bow tie!" shouted Olly.

Daddy put new strings on the puppets,
and showed Olly and Little Owl how to
work them.

Mommy made a
hat and a floppy
tie, and the puppet
looked exactly like
Uncle Horace.

"I know, let's put on *Cinderella* for
Uncle Horace," said Daddy one day.
"As a special thank-you for giving us the
puppets."
They all rehearsed very hard, and then
they invited Uncle Horace to a Special
Performance.

Uncle Horace loved it. "Your prince obviously likes his new hat," he remarked to Little Owl afterward. "He kept it on all through the play."

Some days
later, a
letter arrived.
"Look at this!"
exclaimed Daddy.
"Uncle Horace has
sent us tickets for a
pantomime on
Christmas Eve.
Guess which one!"
"Cinderella!"
yelled Olly.
"How lovely!" said
Mommy.
Little Owl was
very excited.

It seemed a long time until Christmas
Eve. When the day came, they went by
taxi as a special treat.

Little Owl had never been to the theater
before. It was very big.

The curtain went up, and there on the
stage was Cinderella with her broom.
This was the real thing! Little Owl knew
he was going to enjoy it.

When the Ugly Sisters entered, Little
Owl nearly fell off his seat with
astonishment. The tall, elegant one was
Uncle Horace!
So THIS was what
an actor did!

Uncle Horace was really funny, especially dancing with the prince at the Royal Ball.

Little Owl had quite forgotten that the
tall Ugly Sister was Uncle Horace.

He was sorry for
her as she tried to
put on the glass
slipper.

At the end, Little Owl remembered again, and felt very proud as the audience cheered.

Afterward, they went out for supper. When they had almost finished, Little Owl put down his spoon. "Uncle Horace!" he said. "When I grow up, I want to be an actor."

"In that case," replied Uncle Horace, "you had better have your Christmas present now, instead of taking it home for tomorrow."

"Come here, Little
Owl," he said.
From behind his back, he brought out a
hat just like his own, and carefully put it
on Little Owl's head.
Little Owl was thrilled.

There was a beautiful floppy bow tie
too.
"There we are," said Uncle Horace
solemnly. "Little Owl, Honorary
Actor."
"What does 'honorary' mean?" asked
Little Owl.

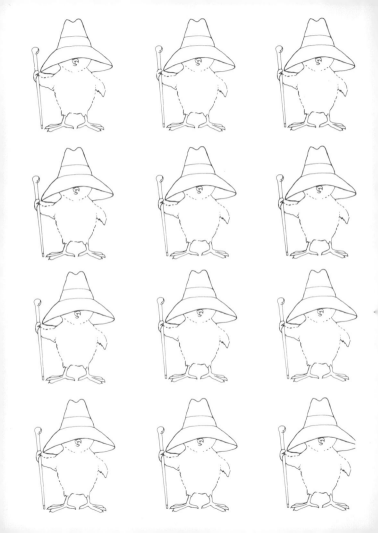